For Susan —**D. U.**
For my grandson Herbie —**T. H.**

Henry Holt and Company, *Publishers since 1866*
Henry Holt® is a registered trademark of Macmillan Publishing Group, LLC.
120 Broadway, New York, NY 10271
mackids.com

Library of Congress Cataloging-in-Publication Data is available.
ISBN 978-1-250-21720-2
Our books may be purchased in bulk for promotional, educational, or business use.
Please contact your local bookseller or the Macmillan Corporate and Premium Sales Department at
(800) 221-7945 ext. 5442 or by email at MacmillanSpecialMarkets@macmillan.com.
First Edition, 2021
Printed in China by RR Donnelley Asia Printing Solutions, Ltd., Dongguan City, Guangdong Province.
The artwork for this book was created using pencil, charcoal, wax crayon, chalk, ink, paper cutouts, and Photoshop.
1 3 5 7 9 10 8 6 4 2

Loving Kindness

Written by
Deborah Underwood

Illustrated by
Tim Hopgood

GODWINBOOKS

HENRY HOLT AND COMPANY • NEW YORK

YOU are a blessing.

You are beautiful just as you are.
You are **loved**, and you **love**.

You make
mistakes,
and it's okay
to make mistakes,
because that's
how you
learn.

You dream. You dance. You breathe the air.

You feel the sun's warmth and admire the cool moon.

You **touch** the **earth,**
the **earth** that **connects** us **all.**

She is a blessing.

She is beautiful just as she is.

She is **loved,** and she **loves.**

She makes mistakes,

and it's okay to make mistakes,

because
that's how
she learns.

She dreams.

She dances.

She breathes the air.

She feels the sun's warmth . . .

and
admires
the cool

moon.

She **touches** the **earth,**
the **earth** that **connects** us **all**.

They are a blessing.

They are beautiful just as they are.

They are loved,

and they love.

They make mistakes,

and it's okay to make mistakes,

because that's how they **learn**.

They **dream.**

They **dance.**

They **breathe** the air.

They **feel** the sun's **warmth**...

and **admire** the cool **moon.**

They **touch** the **earth**,
the **earth** that **connects** us **all**.

Everyone is a blessing.

Everyone is **beautiful** just as they are.
Everyone is **loved**, and everyone loves.

Everyone makes mistakes,
and it's okay to make mistakes,
because that's how we learn.

Everyone **dreams.**
Everyone **dances.**
Everyone **breathes**
the air.

Everyone **feels** the sun's **warmth** …

and **admires** the cool **moon.**

Everyone touches
the earth...

the **earth** that **connects**

us **all.**

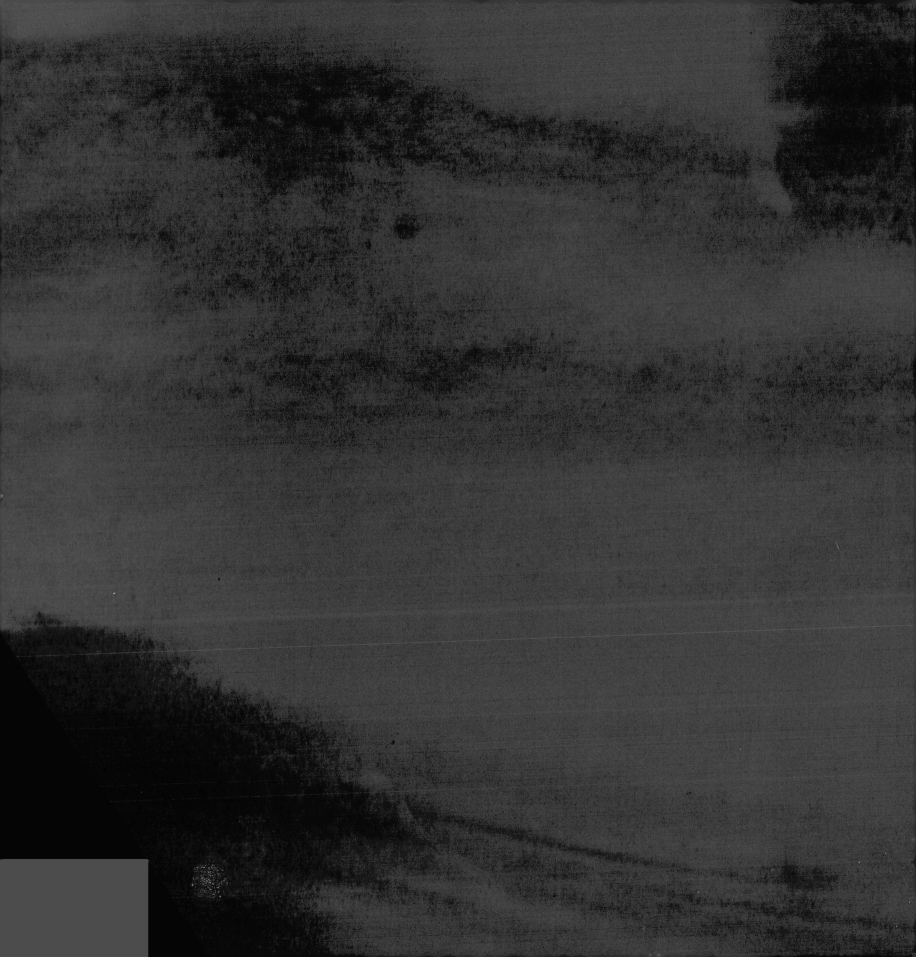